# The RETURN of B.C. rides again

# The RETURN of B.C. rides again

### A B.C. Collection by Johnny Hart

**Andrews and McMeel**
A Universal Press Syndicate Company
**Kansas City • New York**

B.C. is syndicated internationally by Creators Syndicate, Inc.

*The Return of B.C. Rides Again* copyright ©1989 by Creators Syndicate, Inc. All rights reserved. Printed in the United States of America. No part of this book may be used or reproduced in any manner whatsoever without written permission except in the case of reprints in the context of reviews. For information write Andrews and McMeel, a Universal Press Syndicate Company, 4900 Main Street, Kansas City, Missouri 64112.

ISBN: 0-8362-1836-1

Library of Congress Catalog Card Number: 88-83873

6

WHAT GOES:
PINCH,...TEE HEE
PINCH,...TEE HEE
PINCH,..SWAT
I GIVE UP.
A GUY IN AN ELEVATOR WITH 2 GIRLS AND A 'COP IN DRAG.'

HISSSSSSSSSSSSSSS
NOW I WONDER WHAT'S GOT INTO HIM TODAY ?
PROBABLY JUST RAN OVER A NAIL.

bal·der·dash *v.*

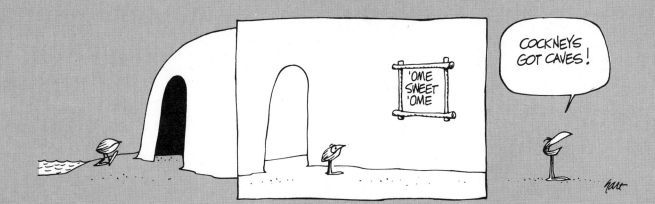

rumble·seat *n.*

42

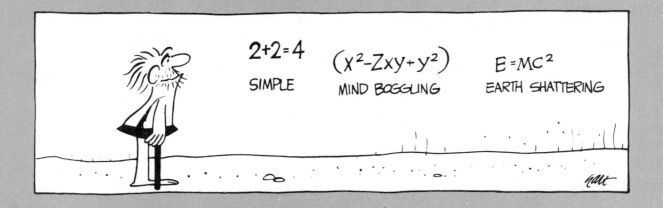

49

54

56

CAMPAIGN PROMISES

I READ WHERE TURTLE MEAT HAS THE DISTINCTIVE FLAVOR OF OTHER MEATS, LIKE...PORK AND VEAL AND CHICKEN...

...EVEN TURKEY.

GET IT IN GEAR, SLUGGO!

COLOR MAN

THE BOOK OF PHRASES

A FORMER COACH WHO WOULD HAVE WON MORE GAMES IF HE HAD STARTED OUT IN THE BOOTH.

THE BOOK OF PHRASES

boot·licker

peace meal

filagree

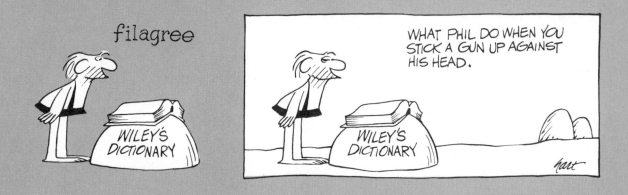

alimentary canal

cur·tail

ilK *n.*

abomination

106

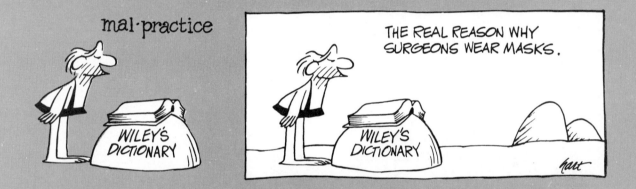

Glut·ton: n

re·cess *n.*